MARION DANE

Alison's Wings

illustrated by ROGER ROTH

Hyperion Books for Children
New York

For my daughter, Beth-Alison
—M. D. B.

Text © 1996 by Marion Dane Bauer.
Illustrations © 1996 by Roger Roth.

Printed in the United States of America.

First Edition
1 3 5 7 9 10 8 6 4 2

The artwork for each picture is prepared using pencil.
This book is set in 20-point Goudy.

Library of Congress Cataloging-in-Publication Data
Bauer, Marion Dane
Alison's wings / Marion Dane Bauer ; illustrated by Roger Roth —
1st ed.
p.   cm.
Summary: Young Alison, dreaming of having her own wings, tries to
find a way to fly.
ISBN 0-7868-0105-0 (trade)—ISBN 0-7868-1121-8 (pbk.)
[1. Wings—Fiction. 2. Flight—Fiction.] I. Roth, Roger, ill.
II. Title.
PZ7.B3262A1   1996
[E]—dc20   95-38772

Table of Contents

Chapter One

All night long, Alison
dreamed of wings.

Big wings.

Beautiful wings.

Wings of her very own.

First there were shoulder bumps. Then the bumps began to itch. Then feathers came poking through.

Alison's wings were damp. Like baby chicks. And curled like new leaves. And kitten soft.

But they reached and reached. They grew long and strong. They pressed against the air.

And Alison flew.

Alison flew higher than her house.

She flew higher than a passing
cloud.

She flew higher than the sun.

"Look!" the leaves on the oak
tree whispered.

"Look!" a brown bird peeped.

"Look!" the wind sang.

"Alison has wings."

And she did!

When Alison awoke, she

hurried to the hall. She stood in front of the long mirror. She turned around and peeked over her shoulder.

There were no wings. No wings at all.

"What are you doing?" her brother asked.

"Looking for my wings," Alison told him.

"Wings!" Mike laughed. "How silly! Girls don't have wings!"

"Birds have wings," Mom said.

"Angels have wings," Dad told Alison.

"Even airplanes have wings," Mike added. "But never girls."

"Then I'll be the first one," Alison said.

11

12

Mike laughed harder.

Even Mom and Dad smiled.

But Alison didn't care. She could see a bump behind each shoulder. That was where her wings would begin.

Chapter Two

Alison sat on the front steps. She sat very still. She sat with her eyes closed. Waiting.

Her shoulder bumps itched. But she didn't scratch. New wings are delicate. Easily discouraged.

Mike banged out the door. "What are you doing?" he asked.

"Nothing," Alison said. And

she squeezed her eyes shut tighter.

Mike didn't move. Alison didn't open her eyes. Now she was waiting for two things. She was waiting for her wings to poke through and for Mike to go away.

"Wings aren't so great," Mike said at last. "There are other ways to fly."

Alison's eyes popped open. "What do you mean?"

Mike held out a towel. "Here," he said. "Try this."

Alison stared at the towel. She stared at Mike.

"Superman flies," Mike said.
"He flies with a cape."
Alison took the towel.

"Superwoman does, too," she said.

She put the towel over her shoulders. She looked back. Her cape was red. It made her feel powerful.

Mike pointed to the porch railing. "You can jump from there," he said.

"Why?" Alison asked.

"If you want to fly, you need a good start."

Alison climbed onto the railing. She spread her red cape. She looked down.

Mom's flowers were below. They
were marigolds. Yellow as the sun.

Nearly as far away as the sun, too.
But Alison had a red cape.

And Mike was watching. So she jumped.

Alison picked herself up. She rubbed her knee. She straightened a squashed marigold.

"Never mind," Mike told her.

"You just need a better start. I'll find you a higher place."

A smile snuck across his mouth.

"Never mind," Alison said. "I like wings better, anyway."

She gave the towel to Mike.

Then she went inside to get a pretty bandage for her knee.

Chapter Three

Alison went next door to show Cindy her bandage. It was purple with pink stars.

She showed Cindy her shoulder bumps, too. "That's where my wings will be," she said.

Cindy said, "I have shoulder bumps. See?" And she showed Alison.

"When your wings come," Alison told her, "we'll fly away together."

"Away where?" Cindy asked.

"Anywhere we like," Alison said.

"Then will we fly back home?" Cindy asked.

"Always," Alison told her.

Cindy smiled. "My uncle Bob flew once," she said. "In a big balloon."

"Really?" Alison was amazed. "Are you sure?"

Cindy nodded. "He flew way up high."

"I wish we had a balloon," Alison said.

Cindy put her hand into her pocket. She pulled out a balloon. She gave it to Alison. "From Rachel's party," she said.

The balloon was blue, as blue as the sky. Alison began to blow.

"Will it be big enough for both of us?" Cindy asked.

"I'll make it big enough," Alison said.

So she blew and blew.

The balloon grew as big as her head. It grew as big as the sun. It

grew as big as the whole sky.

And then it popped.

Bang!

Cindy picked up the scrap of blue. "It's all right," she said. "I didn't really want to fly, anyway."

But Alison did.

Chapter Four

Mom and Dad had a surprise for Alison. A ride in an airplane.

"For a girl who wants wings," they said.

Alison had never been to the airport.

She shook the pilot's hand. She climbed into the plane. The pilot climbed in, too.

Alison looked in front of her. There were levers and dials and lights. She looked behind. There were no more seats.

No seat for Mom. No seat for Dad. Or even for Mike.

"Buckle your seat belt," the pilot said.

She did.

The propeller spun. It spun so fast it disappeared. The engine roared. It roared so loud Alison covered her ears.

"Here we go!" the pilot shouted.

Alison waved to Mom and

Dad and Mike.

Then the airplane rushed
down the runway. It lifted into
the air. And when Alison looked
down, everything was small.

Mom and Dad and Mike.

The airport.

The cars and the trees and even the town.

Alison felt small, too.

The plane hung in the air. Everything else was going away.

This kind of flying might be good for planes, but not for girls.

"I want to go back," she told the pilot.

The plane was too loud. The pilot didn't hear.

So Alison folded her hands in her lap. She sat as still as church. And she waited.

She waited for the airplane
ride to be over.

When they landed, at last,
everyone ran up to the plane.

"Was it fun?" Mike shouted.

"Did you like it?" Mom and Dad asked. Their faces were pink. Their smiles were wide.

"It was nice," Alison said. "Thank you very much." And she smiled politely at them all.

But it wasn't the least bit like having wings.

Chapter Five

Grandpa liked to come to
Alison's house to play.

He and Alison played gin
rummy. Alison always won.

They played baseball.
Sometimes Alison hit the ball
past the lilac bushes. That was a
home run.

They played hide-and-seek.

Grandpa let Alison hide. Every time.

Alison and Grandpa read to each other. They took long walks. And when Alison got stuck in the oak tree, Grandpa climbed up to help her down.

He didn't tell, either.

One morning, Alison was sitting on the front steps. She was sitting very still. She was sitting with her eyes closed. Waiting.

Grandpa came and sat down beside her. "What are you doing?" he asked.

"Waiting for my wings,"
Alison said.

"What kind of wings are you waiting for?" Grandpa asked. "Sparrow wings? Turkey wings? Eagle wings?"

"Girl wings," Alison told him.

Grandpa nodded wisely. "The very best kind," he said.

So he made her a swing of rope and board. He hung it in the oak tree on the hill. And he said, "Here you are. Wings for a girl."

"Oh, Grandpa," Alison said. "How silly!" But she sat on the swing.

"Push off," Grandpa said.

38

Alison pushed. The hill fell away.

Alison touched the ground again.

She swung higher than her house.

She swung higher than a passing cloud.

She swung higher than the sun.

It was almost like flying.

But when the swing stopped, Alison reached back to feel. She still had shoulder bumps.

But no wings.

"Nothing yet?" Grandpa asked.

"Nothing yet," Alison told him. "But it's the nicest swing in the world."

Chapter Six

Alison lay in bed. "I wish I had

wings," she sighed to the cozy dark.

The dark made no reply.

"Girl wings," she whispered.

"So I could fly," she added, just

before she slipped into sleep. Just
before she began to dream.

She dreamed about shoulder
bumps. She dreamed the bumps
began to itch. She dreamed
feathers came poking through.

Alison's wings were damp.
Like baby chicks. And curled like
new leaves. And kitten soft.

But they reached and reached.
They grew long and strong. They
pressed against the air.

And Alison flew.

Alison flew higher than her
house.

Alison flew higher than a passing cloud.

She flew higher than the sun.

"Look!" the leaves on the oak tree whispered.

"Look!" a brown bird peeped.
"Look!" the wind sang.
"Alison has wings."
And she did!